JE
Smath, Jerry.
What Daddy loves

MID-CONTINENT PUBLIC LIBRARY
Liberty Branch
1000 Kent Street
Liberty, MO 64068

LI

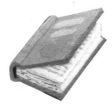

What Daddy Loves

illustrated by Jerry Smath
written by Sue Kassirer

WITHDRAWN
FROM THE RECORDS
MID-CONTINENT PUB

Reader's Digest Children's Books™

Pleasantville, New York • Bath, United Kingdom • Montréal, Québec

My daddy's the best. When I see him coming home from work, I run down the street—fast!—and jump in his arms. Then he loves to whirl me around and around in the air.

I love it, too.

MID-CONTINENT PUBLIC LIBRARY

3 0001 00930622 8

MID-CONTINENT PUBLIC LIBRARY
Liberty Branch
1000 Kent Street
Liberty, MO 64068

LI

Daddy loves to plop down in his big red armchair and read the paper.

I love reading it, too.

Daddy loves to cook. He makes the best spaghetti you've ever had! Mommy's spaghetti is good, but Daddy's is *scrumptilicious*!

I love cooking—and eating—spaghetti, too.

Daddy loves going on hikes. He always reminds me that we still have to walk all the way back, but I never listen.

I love going on hikes, too.

Daddy loves taking me to his office. Everyone's always so glad to see me. It's like they've never seen a kid before! And there's tons of stuff to do. Daddy needs lots of help.

I love going there, too.

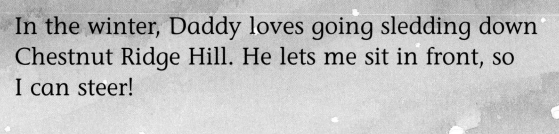

In the winter, Daddy loves going sledding down Chestnut Ridge Hill. He lets me sit in front, so I can steer!

I love going sledding, too.

In the spring, Daddy loves planting the garden.
First he turns the soil and then he sprinkles the seeds.

I love planting the garden, too.

In the summer, Daddy loves fishing. He likes to go really early in the morning—even before Mommy is up!

I love fishing, too.

On clear summer nights, Daddy loves gazing at the stars. We sit on the old blue comforter and stare up at the whole wide sky.

I love gazing at the stars, too.

In the fall, Daddy loves raking up the leaves and putting them in great, big piles. We're really lucky— I think we have more leaves than anyone else on the block!

I love raking up the leaves, too.

All year long, Daddy loves fixing things around the house. "If it's not one thing, it's another," says Daddy.

I love fixing things, too.

There are so many things Daddy loves. But most of all…

...Daddy loves me.